DANGER! ACTION! TROUBLE! ADVENTURE!

THE DATA SET

A Case of the Clones

By Ada Hopper   Illustrated by Sam Ricks

LITTLE SIMON
New York London Toronto Sydney New Delhi

LITTLE SIMON

An imprint of Simon & Schuster Children's Publishing Division

1230 Avenue of the Americas, New York, New York 10020

First Little Simon paperback edition September 2016

Copyright © 2016 by Simon & Schuster, Inc.

All rights reserved, including the right of reproduction in whole or in part in any form. LITTLE SIMON is a registered trademark of Simon & Schuster, Inc., and associated colophon is a trademark of Simon & Schuster, Inc. For information about special discounts for bulk purchases, please contact Simon & Schuster Special Sales at 1-866-506-1949 or business@simonandschuster.com. The Simon & Schuster Speakers Bureau can bring authors to your live event. For more information or to book an event contact the Simon & Schuster Speakers Bureau at 1-866-248-3049 or visit our website at www.simonspeakers.com.

Designed by John Daly. The text of this book was set in Serifa.

Manufactured in the United States of America 0816 MTN

10 9 8 7 6 5 4 3 2 1

Cataloging-in-Publication Data is available for this title from the Library of Congress.

ISBN 978-1-4814-7114-5 (hc)
ISBN 978-1-4814-7113-8 (pbk)
ISBN 978-1-4814-7115-2 (eBook)

CONTENTS

Chapter 1 The Ultimate Pick-Me-Up   7

Chapter 2 Nuttier Than a Nut Bar   19

Chapter 3 100 Percent Confused   27

Chapter 4 Playing Tricks   41

Chapter 5 Strange Encounters of the DATA
Set Kind   55

Chapter 6 Double Trouble   67

Chapter 7 Catch the Clones   79

Chapter 8 Don't Touch Those Snacks!   91

Chapter 9 Questions Answered   101

Chapter 10 Always Time for Team Time   113

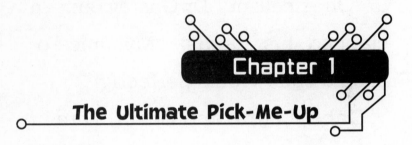

Chapter 1

The Ultimate Pick-Me-Up

"Mmmmm. I taste cranberry and pumpkin . . . ," Cesar said as he took another gulp of juice. "With a hint of turkey gravy."

"No way. Something's wrong with your taste buds," said Laura. "It tastes like peach cobbler."

"You're both wrong," said Gabriel.

"This is totally a banana milk shake."

"Oh, excellent!" Dr. Gustav Bunsen clapped his hands. "My Juice-o-Tronic 2000 works perfectly!"

Gabe, Laura, and Cesar were in Dr. Bunsen's laboratory, helping him test his newest invention,

when they should have been doing their homework. But Dr. Bunsen insisted that they try his perfect "pick-me-up" drinks to boost their energy. It was going to be a busy day.

Cesar tasted his juice again. "I don't get it," he said. "Mine tastes like Thanksgiving dinner."

"Precisely!" Bunsen said. "The Juice-o-Tronic 2000 makes juice that tastes like whatever you are craving. Mine, for example, tastes like grilled salmon and brussels sprouts!" The doctor took a big gulp.

"Yuck!" cried Laura.

The boys and Dr. Bunsen laughed.

"Well, thanks for the refreshing but weird drink, Dr. B.," said Gabe. "Now we need to go to Olive's house."

"Ah, yes, Olive Thompson. Where *is* the newest member of the DATA Set?" Dr. Bunsen asked.

"She's sick," Laura explained. "Cesar took notes for her."

Cesar tapped his head. "Yep. "Photographic memory. Come on, guys. After Olive's, I have to do homework *and* clean my room. It's

so messy, I can't even find my emergency brain-food snacks in there anymore."

"That's nothing," said Laura. "I have to do my homework *and* finish building my latest invention *and* patch up the tree house roof. You may not be able to find your snacks at home, Cesar, but the squirrels sure found your snacks at the tree house. They chewed a hole right through the roof!"

"Oh no!" Cesar gasped. "Don't tell me my homemade fruit and nut bars are—"

"Gone," Laura finished for him. "Reduced to crumbs."

Cesar groaned. "Aw, now I need to make more." He sighed. "Add another thing to my to-do list!"

"Well, I've got you both beat," bragged Gabe. "I have to do my homework, clean my room, finish my chores, *and* paint posters for

the bake sale and the Science Quiz Bowl."

"My, my, what three busy DATA Set squirrels you are!" Dr. Bunsen said. "Speaking of which, I have one more invention to show you. I've tested it on, well, squirrels, and the results—"

"Sorry, Dr. B.," Gabe interrupted. "But we really do have to go."

"Maybe next time," said Cesar as he took the last sip of his juice.

The doctor waved good-bye disappointedly as the DATA Set hurried out the door. Then he eyed their empty juice glasses.

Chapter 2

Nuttier Than a Nut Bar

"Thanks for bringing me my homework," Olive said as her friends walked into her room. She was sitting in her pajamas. A pile of tissues filled the wastebasket next to her bed.

"How are you feeling?" Cesar asked.

Olive blew her nose. "Better. It's just a cold now. I'll be back at school tomorrow."

"That's good," said Cesar. "It's been crazy in class. Mrs. Bell is on a homework rampage."

"I can tell!" Olive glanced over Cesar's notes. "There must be thirty pages here. You sure this isn't the teacher's edition?"

Cesar grinned proudly.

Meanwhile, Laura was walking around Olive's room. "You've got a lot of cool stuff in here."

"Yeah, what's that fancy award for?" Gabe pointed to a framed certificate.

"Oh, I competed in the Teslaville Prep Mathematics Bowl," Olive said.

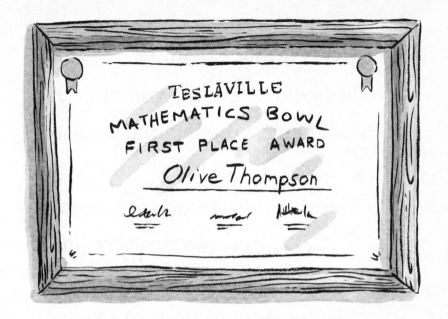

TESLAVILLE
MATHEMATICS BOWL
FIRST PLACE AWARD
Olive Thompson

Gabe looked closer at the award. "Olive, you didn't just compete. You won first place!"

Olive coughed. "Yeah, kind of."

"More like kind of great!" Cesar was impressed. "You're a math genius!"

Olive blushed.

"We should hang out in your room more often," Laura said, admiring an antique radio on Olive's bookshelf. "You have good taste. I built a radio not too long ago. It led me to an alien. I'll tell you about it sometime."

"Speaking of taste . . ." Cesar hurried over to Olive's desk. "Energy nut bars! All right!"

Olive giggled as Cesar helped himself to one. She looked at the stack of notes again and was suddenly overwhelmed. "I don't know how I'm going to catch up on all this homework."

"Don't worry," said Cesar, munching away. "We're all behind. I'm telling you, Mrs. Bell has gone nuts. Nuttier than this nut bar!"

"Speaking of which, we should head home," said Laura.

"Here." Cesar handed Olive one of her snacks. "You need an energy boost more than any of us. See you at school tomorrow?"

Olive smiled. "You can count on it."

Chapter 3

100 Percent Confused

The next morning Olive arrived at school early. When she bounded into the classroom, Cesar was sitting at one of the desks.

"Hey!" Olive waved to her friend. "How come you're here already?"

"I am not programmed to be late," Cesar replied.

Olive paused. Cesar was acting very strange. "But aren't you always late because your mom cooks you a big breakfast?"

Cesar didn't reply. He stared at the blackboard instead.

Olive followed his gaze. "Oh, you must be memorizing the homework assignment for tonight!

Thanks again for your notes. They were a huge help." She searched through her backpack and pulled out an energy nut bar. "Here, I brought this to say thank you."

"I do not need that," he said.

"Wow! Are you okay?" Olive asked disappointedly. "I've never heard you say no to a snack before."

"I am not hungry."

Olive's mouth dropped open. "Cesar Garcia Moreno? Not hungry? Are you joking? I mean, first, you are never early to school and second . . ."

Before she could finish, Cesar stood up. "Lesson learned. I am never early to school," he said in a

flat voice. Then he marched out of the classroom.

"Gee," she said, looking down at the nut bar. "I really thought he would like this."

Just then students began filing through the door. Mrs. Bell came in too, and clunked down extra-thick assignment packets on her desk.

"Hey, Olive!" Gabe called as he and Laura walked inside. "How are you feeling?"

"Okay," said Olive. "Have you guys seen Cesar this morning?"

"That's my name; don't wear it out," Cesar interrupted as he entered the classroom holding a half-eaten banana.

Olive looked at him in surprise. "I thought you weren't hungry." Then she noticed his blue shirt. "And why did you change?"

Cesar raised an eyebrow.

"Oh, Olive, you know me. I'll never change."

"Seriously." Gabe chuckled. "Cesar's always hungry!"

"It's true," Cesar said with his

mouth full. "Oh, are you going to eat that energy bar?"

"But I just saw you sitting over there." Olive pointed to Cesar's empty desk. "You were wearing a green shirt. And you said you weren't hungry."

Laura looked at Olive. "Hey, are
you sure you're feeling better?"

She felt Olive's forehead and compared it to hers.

Did I really just imagine talking to Cesar? thought Olive. "Hmmm, maybe I'm not one hundred percent better yet," she said. Olive asked Mrs. Bell if she could go

see the school nurse. As she left the classroom, Olive was certain about one thing. She may not be 100 percent better, but she sure was 100 percent confused.

Chapter 4

Playing Tricks

As Olive walked to the nurse's office, students rushed past her to get to class on time. Everyone darted left and right into open classroom doors until, finally, there was only one other student left in the hall. He was tacking up posters.

Olive blinked. It was Gabe!

"Gabe?" she asked, coming up behind him. "Why aren't you back in class?"

Gabe didn't turn around. "I am supposed to hang bake sale posters," he said.

Olive studied his outfit. "I could

have sworn you were wearing a red sweatshirt," she murmured.

Two straggling students raced by. "We're gonna be late!" one of them cried.

"Wait," the other student, Ben, said. "Hey, Gabe, I need your help with the extra-credit question

from Mrs. Bell's homework. Are dinosaurs related to chickens? What's the answer?"

Gabe tacked up another poster. "I am not supposed to know this," he said.

The boys and Olive stood there, shocked.

"Dude, Mrs. Bell's homework stumped Gabe from the DATA Set!" Ben exclaimed as he and his friend sprinted off to class.

Olive turned to Gabe. "You know the answer, but you didn't want to cheat, right?" she said.

"I mean, you know everything about dinosaurs, right?"

"I know the posters need to be hung," Gabe said stiffly. "Please do not interrupt."

"Oh—I . . . ," Olive stammered. She didn't mean to *bother* him.

"Sorry," she said quietly.

Gabe picked up a new stack of posters and walked away.

Olive frowned. Now two of her friends were acting really strange.

At the nurse's office, Ms. Phillips took Olive's temperature. After a few more tests, the nurse told her everything seemed normal, and sent Olive back to class.

"I don't think anything seems normal today," Olive mumbled as she left.

When Olive returned, Mrs. Bell was going over the extra-credit question on the homework assignment.

"And finally," Mrs. Bell said. She looked at Gabe. "I'm assuming you'd like to answer this one, Mr. Martinez?"

Gabe grinned. "You bet! Dinosaurs *are* related to chickens."

"That's correct," said Mrs. Bell. "Well done!"

Olive glanced at Ben. He was giving Gabe an odd look.

"Gabe," Olive whispered. "Why did you pretend to not know the answer before?"

"What are you talking about?" Gabe asked.

"The dinosaurs and chickens," Olive said. "You said you didn't know the answer."

Gabe made a funny face. "Me? Not know an answer about dinosaurs? Not to brag, but I know everything about dinosaurs."

"I think even the dinosaurs know that," whispered Laura. "And they're extinct!"

Gabe, Laura, and Cesar laughed,

but Olive's face fell. She didn't think the joke was funny at all.

So much for a warm welcome back, thought Olive.

Chapter 5

Strange Encounters of the
DATA Set Kind

After school Olive hid under the
jungle gym—alone. She had avoided
her friends for the rest of the day. It
wasn't nice of them to play a trick
on her—pretending they hadn't
seen her or talked to her when they
clearly had. She suddenly missed

her old friends back in Teslaville.

Then another kid appeared in front of her.

Olive yelped. It was Laura!

"You shouldn't sneak up on people like that," Olive exclaimed.

Laura ignored her. She opened a toolbox and began tinkering with the jungle gym.

"I guess you're pretending you don't see me too," Olive said shortly.

Laura still didn't reply. She unbolted a bar from the jungle gym.

"What are you doing?" Olive asked.

"I must remove the support beams," Laura answered.

"Why?"

"I must repair the tree house," she responded.

Olive looked up at the towering jungle gym full of kids. "Wait! What if that's part of a load-bearing slide? This whole playground could collapse without it!"

Laura paused and said, "Negative." Then she took apart the bars and carried them away.

"Hold up!" Olive called, but Laura ran around the school out of sight. Olive was in shock. Playing a trick on her was one thing, but this was going too far. "Something's not right. I need to get help."

Then she turned and ran—right

smack into Gabe, Laura, and Cesar!

"Whoa, Olive, slow down!" exclaimed Laura.

Olive stared at Laura. She felt like her head was spinning. "How are you here? I *just* saw you under the jungle gym."

"What are you talking about?" Laura asked. "We came to find *you*."

"We've barely seen you all day," said Cesar. "Is something going on?"

Olive had had it with their jokes. "This isn't funny anymore. First off, when I saw Cesar early this morning, I offered him an energy nut bar, but he didn't want it."

"I *WHAT*?" cried Cesar. "I would never do that! I actually dreamed about those bars last night. *Dreamed about them!*"

"And then I saw Gabe putting up bake sale posters in the hallway," Olive continued. "Ben saw you there too. He asked you about the dinosaur extra-credit question, but you didn't know the answer."

Gabe scratched his head. "Whoever you saw in the hallway definitely wasn't me. I wondered who put up those posters—they stole my job!"

Olive shook her head. "I'm *sure* it was you. And then just now—"

Laura interrupted her. "Let me guess. You saw *me*."

Olive nodded. "You took the jungle gym apart!"

"Hmmm," said Laura. "So Cesar refused food, Gabe didn't know the answer to a dinosaur question, and I apparently took apart the jungle gym? Guys, are you picking up on a pattern here?"

"Bunsen!" the friends moaned.

Chapter 6

Double Trouble

"Well, of course it was me!" The doctor rummaged around his lab while the DATA Set watched.

"But how did you make doubles of us?" Laura asked.

"And why?" added Gabe.

Dr. Bunsen searched through a delivery crate as he explained.

"It was quite simple! My *other* latest invention, which I wanted to show you yesterday, is the Clone-o-Matic. It can instantly replicate anything. I—shoo, Oscar!" The doctor batted away a curious squirrel nosing into the crate.

Dr. Bunsen adjusted his goggles. "I used the DNA from your juice glasses to make exact replicas of you. You were so busy, I thought extra hands might do the trick."

"Oh, it did the trick all right," said Olive. "It tricked me into thinking Gabe, Laura, and Cesar were making fun of me!"

"Making fun?" the doctor asked, puzzled. "But that seems unlike— OSCAR, I TOLD YOU TO WAIT!"

The squirrel scurried away as the doctor closed his oversized pantry doors.

Dr. Bunsen sighed. "Since I've tested my Clone-o-Matic on squirrels, I'm afraid I've created some extra-hungry friends."

"Here, try these." Olive held out her box of energy nut bars. Oscar the squirrel leaped up and snatched a bar away before Dr. Bunsen could even take it.

"Aw," said Cesar. "Those were mine."

"So is there a way to un-clone the clones?" asked Gabe.

"Of course!" said the doctor. "I simply need to hit the reverse button. Though, we must find the clones first."

Laura grinned. "If they're our doubles, there's only one place we'd be."

The DATA Set and Dr. Bunsen went to Laura's superawesome tree house. Sure enough, there were the clones! Clone-Cesar was doing homework. Clone-Gabe was painting more signs. And Clone-Laura was patching the hole in the roof.

"All right, my young friends," said Dr. Bunsen as he lifted the Clone-o-Matic. *"Huzzah!"*

There was a bright flash as the doctor set off the device.

When the light faded, everyone looked around.

"Did it work?" asked Olive.

"Oh, dear, oh, dear, oh, double dear," said Dr. Bunsen as he shook his head. Across the room there were six clones instead of three!

"Um, maybe my math is off, but why are there even more of us now?" cried Cesar.

"The Clone-o-Matic was set to Double the Trouble instead of—"

Before Bunsen could finish, the clones scattered away!

"Quick, Dr. B.!" cried Gabe. "Undouble them!"

"I'm afraid my invention can't handle this many clones at once," Dr. Bunsen said. "I'll need to recharge it."

"So what do we do?" asked Cesar. "The world isn't ready for three of me!"

"Never fear!" cried the doctor. "I'll be back on the double! In the meantime, just keep *your* doubles out of trouble!"

As Dr. Bunsen hurried away, the DATA Set looked at one another.

"Wait. If the clones are doing our chores," said Laura, "that means they're heading . . ."

"Home," finished Gabe. "We have to stop them before our parents see them!"

Chapter 7

Catch the Clones

Gabe was outside his house when he saw the first clone in his bedroom. "Oh, great. He's inside already!"

As he bolted up the stairs, his mother caught him by surprise. "Gabe? I thought I heard you up here. How was school today?"

"It was, um . . . crowded," Gabe said nervously. His clone was already busy tidying up under his bed.

Gabe closed the door slightly. "I'm, uh, pretty tired. . . . I think I might lie down for a bit," he said as he rushed into his room.

"Gabriel," said his mother. "I believe

you are forgetting something."

Gabe poked his head out into the hall. "Um . . ."

"You promised to rake the leaves in the front yard," his mom said. "You have to do all your chores."

"Oh, right! Hold on. I just need to change into my leaf-sweeping shirt."

CLATTER! CRASH! The clone dropped something on the floor.

"*¡Ay dios mio!*" cried his mother. "What was that?"

"Nothing!" claimed Gabe. "One of my books fell off the shelf." Gabe looked around his room in horror. The clone was dusting his

fossil replicas—and knocking them down one by one!

Gabe chased his clone around the room, picking up the mess. Then there was a noise outside.

WHIRRRRRRRRR.

"Oh no," Gabe groaned.

His second clone was out front

with the leaf blower. This was a disaster! He had to stop the clones before his mom saw that there were two too many Gabes!

"Please," Gabe begged. "Stop dusting!"

"I am programmed to dust," the clone replied.

CLATTER! CRASH! CLATTER!

Three more fossil replicas toppled off the shelf.

Gabe grabbed his hair in frustration. "You're breaking all my stuff!"

"I am programmed to dust," the clone repeated.

CRASH!

Gabe's favorite dinosaur lamp

fell to the floor and shattered.

"No!" cried Gabe.

"Is everything all right in there, *mi hijo*?" called Gabe's mom.

"Uh . . . yeah, Mom!" Gabe answered.

WHIRRRRRRR. The leaf blower grew louder and louder.

Gabe needed to get outside before his mom noticed.

"Please stop!" Gabe pleaded with the clone. "If you *have* to work, then why don't you . . . rake leaves instead!"

The clone immediately stopped. "Is the work of raking leaves more important than the work of cleaning this room?"

"You bet!" exclaimed Gabe.

"Very well," said the clone.

Gabe breathed a sigh of relief.

Phew, finally, he thought. *That was close. Now, how do I get them out of here?*

Chapter 8

Don't Touch Those Snacks!

Meanwhile, over at Cesar's house, things were *not* going any better.

"No, no, no!" Cesar cried as his clone dumped all his brain-food snacks into garbage bags. "Why are you throwing away all my stuff?"

"The room must be cleaned,"

replied the clone. "Food must be thrown away."

"THAT IS THE CRAZIEST THING I'VE EVER HEARD MYSELF SAY!" yelled Cesar, clinging to his last box of crackers for dear life.

"Sweetie pie!" Cesar's mom called. She was in the kitchen

cooking dinner. "Where's my little dumpling?"

Cesar left his clone and raced into the kitchen. "I'm right here, Mom!"

"Oh, there's my little sugar plum." She was stirring a bubbling pot of gravy on the stovetop. "Dinner will be ready in fifteen minutes. I made your favorite—a Thanksgiving meal with all the sides!"

"I do not require food," a clone called from the study.

"What did you say, sweetie?" Cesar's mom asked.

Cesar thought fast. "I said . . . mmmm, I can't wait for food!"

Suddenly, the phone rang.

Cesar grabbed it. "Hello?"

"Hello," echoed the first Clone-Cesar. He had answered the upstairs phone in Cesar's room. "Clone-Cesar's house, how can I help you?"

"Hello," the second Clone-Cesar repeated from the phone in the study.

Cesar clutched his head. "How many phones do we have in this house!"

"Cesar, is that you?" It was Gabe on the other end.

"You bet," said Cesar. "But hang on a second, will you?"

The real Cesar hurried into the study and upstairs to wrestle the phones away from the clones. "All three of me, at your service," he told Gabe.

"Listen, I figured out how to get the clones to come back to the tree

house," Gabe explained urgently. "Tell them you need to rake the leaves there. With new work to do, they will run over here."

"Roger that," said Cesar.

Suddenly he heard the vacuum cleaner starting up.

"Must clean pages out of books," the clone said.

"No, no, nooooooo!" cried Cesar, dropping the phone and trying to save his favorite books before they were sucked up into the vacuum and destroyed forever.

Chapter 9

Questions Answered

"Got it, thanks," Laura said as she hung up the phone and turned to Olive. "That was Gabe. We need to get the clones back to the tree house."

"Okay, good," said Olive. She watched as Laura's clones busily attempted to complete several unfinished inventions on the garage floor. "That's if we can get their attention. They won't even look at us."

Laura couldn't help smiling. "They're in the *invention zone*, just like me."

"That reminds me," said Olive. "Once we un-clone the clones, we need to put the jungle gym back together."

"You got it," said Laura. Then she paused. "Why were you hanging out there all alone, by the way?"

"I told you, I thought you were playing a trick on me."

"So you decided to give us the silent treatment?" Laura said. "How come you didn't just ask us what was going on?"

Olive was quiet for a minute. "I don't know. I thought maybe you didn't like me anymore."

"What?" Laura exclaimed. "Now you're the one

who sounds crazy. Have you seen how excited Cesar gets when you come into class? And Gabe is totally impressed by how quick you are with numbers. And for me, it's great having another girl in our group."

Olive smiled and was about to say something when one of Laura's inventions started making whirring noises. "Is it supposed to do that?" Olive asked.

A glint came to the clones' eyes. "Superpowered static generator is operational."

"Uh-oh . . . ," said Laura.

"What does *that* mean?" asked Olive.

"It was for Cesar's birthday party," Laura explained, backing away. "I wanted to create enough static electricity to attach balloons all over his house. But I never got the prototype to work."

"But if it works . . . ," said Olive.

"Then we're gonna get zapped!" screamed Laura.

A minute later Laura, Olive, and both clones shuffled out of the garage. Their hair was superstaticky, sizzled, and standing on end in all directions.

"That was shocking," said Olive as her clothes crackled with static electricity.

The clones stood at attention. "Next task, please," they said in unison.

"Go to the tree house for your

next assignment," said a frizzled-
looking Laura. "And remind me

to really think through all my
inventions in the future."

Chapter 10

Always Time for Team Time

Gabe and Cesar waited in front of the tree house. Their clones were hard at work raking leaves into a giant pile.

"Where are they?" Gabe asked. "Laura and Olive should have been here by now."

As soon as he spoke, Laura and

Olive came running up with the clones behind them.

"What happened to you guys?" Gabe stared at the girls. "Your hair looks like you've been zapped by lightning."

Laura grumbled, "Don't ask."

Just then Dr. Bunsen arrived with the recharged Clone-o-Matic.

"Did someone say 'zap'?" he asked. "Get ready to zap things back to normal. Look out, kids!"

"Wait!" cried Olive. "Look at the clones. They're running all over the place!"

She was right. The clones were busy arguing over who would rake the leaves.

"We must work," insisted Gabe's clones. "We are programmed to rake the leaves."

"We must rake all the leaves," said Laura's clones. "We must make a new pile."

"We must relocate the leaves to a new area," said Cesar's doubles.

The clones kept undoing one

another's work in order to finish the job. But instead of lending a helping hand, they were making an even bigger mess.

"I wish these clones would stand still," said Bunsen. "I had an easier time herding squirrels!"

Then Olive had an idea. "Dr. Bunsen, I can calculate the perfect mathematical angle to aim the beam so they're all caught at once. We just need to wait until they are on the same side of the lawn."

"Oh, how clever!" exclaimed the doctor. He handed Olive the Clone-o-Matic, and she climbed up to a high tree branch.

"And don't forget the magic word!" added the doctor.

Olive did a quick calculation and then she cried, *"Huzzah!"* With a bright flash, the Clone-o-Matic went *ZAP!*

Everyone closed their eyes to avoid the burst of light. When they opened them again, the clones were gone.

"Did it work?" asked Laura. "Are we clone free?"

Rustle. Rustle. Crunch.

One by one, six little squirrels popped up out of the leaves.

"Are those . . . our clones?" Gabe asked as he looked at two of the squirrels that were wearing tiny glasses.

"Hmmmmm," said Dr. Bunsen as he scratched his head. "I suppose this *could* be the side effect of having cloned so many squirrels."

Gabe raised an eyebrow. "What do we do? Just let them go?"

The squirrels blinked at Gabe, then scampered away.

"I guess so," said Cesar.

Everyone watched the squirrels

clamber up the tree, into the tree
house, and back out through the
window. Cesar's clone squirrel
clutched an energy bar tightly in
its mouth.

"Looks like he found the last
one," said Laura.

"A squirrel after my own heart," declared Cesar.

"We did it!" Olive shouted excitedly as she climbed down from the tree. "Newtonburg is officially clone free!"

Laura put an arm around Olive's shoulders. "We sure did. And it's all thanks to you."

"Indeed!" said Dr. Bunsen. "But before you go, I have another new invention that I'd like to show you—"

"No!" the kids yelled together.

"I mean . . . we should head home. Besides, my room is an even bigger mess now," said Gabe.

"And Olive and I have to fix the jungle gym," said Laura.

"And I have to replace my entire brain-food snack supply!" said Cesar. His stomach rumbled loudly.

"Ugh, all this running around has left me starving. Do you guys want to come over to eat? My mom made my favorite turkey dinner and she always makes extras. No matter how busy we are, there's always time for a turkey dinner, right?"

"Sounds great, but only if I can get *seconds*!" said Olive with a smile.

THE DATA SET

FOR MORE DANGER! ACTION!
TROUBLE! ADVENTURE!
Visit thedatasetbooks.com

Little
Simon